To Iris and Penelope

Dr. Vivian

For Liana, Peter,
Cara and Daniel

Thank You
for
Giraffes

Vivian Husnik

Child Wonder Press

My daughter Cara loves giraffes. When she was two years old, she always included giraffes in her prayers. One evening her usually long list of blessings ran a little short. Her prayer went something like this: "Thank You for my home. Thank You for my family. Thank You for our food. Thank You for giraffes. . . . . and more giraffes." After she heard me tell this story to several people, that phrase became part of every night's prayer.

My prayer is that all children, to whomever they pray, have much for which to be thankful. VH

thank you for giraffes

and more giraffes

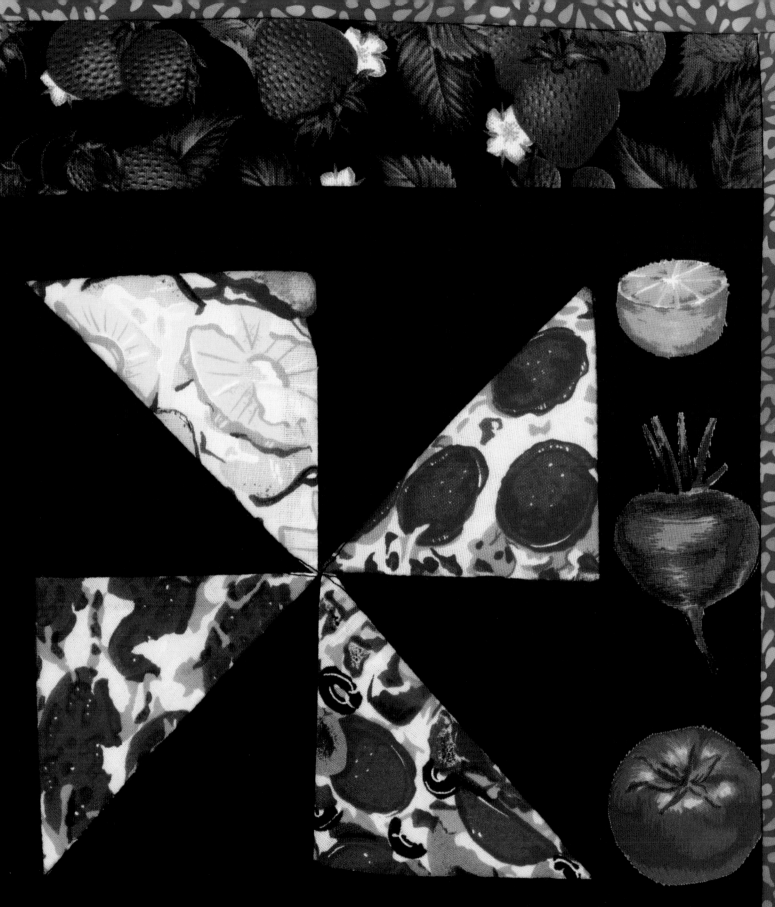

thank you for food

thank you for water,
and otters

thank you for wild

thank you for calm

thank you for sunsets

thank you for dawn

thank you for home . . .

. . . and places far

thank you for the moon and stars

thank you for animals big . . .

. . . and small

but most
of all,

thank you
for love

Printed in Hong Kong
Book Design: Budget Book Design
This is a BooksJustBooks.com book

For information on obtaining more copies,
and to contact the author,
please write to:

1608 Merrill Street
St. Paul, MN 55108

childwonderpress.com